8's or 4's?

Welcome to the Trap

La'kendrick Davis

Bulk & Community Sales

Interested in ordering this book in larger quantities for your school, youth program, or organization? We offer **bulk discounts** for orders of **10 or more copies**, with special pricing for educational institutions, churches, libraries, and community outreach initiatives.

Let this story spark important conversations about identity, choices, and legacy in the lives of young readers. Whether it's for a classroom set, a book club, or a mentorship curriculum—this book is designed to inspire, educate, and connect.

To request a quote or custom bundle (including author visits, discussion guides, or signed copies), visit us at **linktr.ee/8sor4s.**

Table of Contents

Prologue: The Aftermath

Six Months Later

The streets felt different now.

Lil' Q stood on the corner of 45th and Maple, staring at what used to be **Carter's Convenience.** The store was boarded up, its once-familiar red and white sign now faded and stained with graffiti. The makeshift memorial out front—a cluster of candles, wilted flowers, and handwritten notes—told the story of a community in mourning.

"Rest in Peace, Mr. Carter."
"Justice for Tasha."
"Who protects our own?"

The air was thick with something Lil' Q couldn't name—anger, grief, maybe even fear.

The shooting had changed everything.

The block was quieter now, but not in a peaceful way. People didn't hang out like they used to. Parents rushed their kids inside before the streetlights flickered on. Folks looked over their shoulders more, whispers spreading faster than the wind.

The **8s and 4s** were at each other's throats.

Everyone knew it was Marcus and his crew that hit the store, but the 4s weren't about to take the fall for a job that got an **innocent girl shot and a respected man killed.**

The streets were about to explode.

Lil' Q clenched his jaw, shoving his hands deep into his pockets. He didn't want to be here, but he couldn't stay away. Not when the whole neighborhood was still bleeding from what happened.

From what *Marcus* did.

"*You keep comin' back here like it'll bring him back,*" April's voice broke through his thoughts.

Lil' Q turned to see her standing a few feet away, her hood pulled up, arms crossed tight against the evening chill. Her eyes were tired. They all were.

"*I don't know what I'm doin',*" he admitted. "*Just don't feel right, actin' like life's normal.*"

April sighed, stepping up beside him. "*Ain't nothin' normal anymore.*"

They stood in silence for a moment, both staring at the boarded-up store, the memory of that night playing on loop in their minds.

Then April asked the question that had been burning in both of them since the shooting.

"*You think he's still out there?*"

Lil' Q didn't have to ask who she meant.

Marcus.

The boy who used to be their friend.

The boy who was now **a ghost in his own neighborhood.**

Lil' Q exhaled slowly. "*Yeah. He out there.*"

April swallowed. "*Then it isn't over.*"

"*No*," Lil' Q said, voice firm, gaze locked on the empty streets ahead.

"*It ain't.*"

And when Marcus comes back… he knew the streets wouldn't be so forgiving.

Chapter 1:
Welcome to *The Nawth*

May 2025 - Benton Heights, Mississippi

Twelve-year-old Quin Washington was known in his neighborhood as "Lil' Q," - a name he carried from his old neighborhoods. Now, again, Lil' Q had been uprooted and relocated to another tight-knit African American and Latino community where *everyone* knew *everyone* else's business.

The Nawth (North), as they called it, was a place where during the day you could find kids playing basketball and slap boxing in the streets. You could hear music blaring from car windows from young drivers trying to impress the neighborhood. Then of course, there are the grandmas (aka "The Porch Patrol") sitting out daily on their porches like they were clocking in for a job, keeping an eye on **everything**. But by the time the streetlights came on, all the kids were rushed inside by their parents. At night in this hood, you'd also find strays walking the streets looking for their next hits, local clicks breaking into homes while the owners worked at night, or random house parties on any given day of the week that the entire neighborhood could hear.

Lil' Q's block, Carter & 40th street, was the center of his universe, subconsciously molding and shaping him in unimaginable ways he didn't realize.

Even though he was only twelve, he had seen more than most kids his age. Memories of chalked out bodies from one neighborhood to the other, of kids his own age haunted him, as he questioned why he had been sentenced to this kind of life.

Lil' Q's dad left when he was eight years old and that's when they begin traveling from neighborhood to neighborhood, from school to school. That's when his mom started to work two jobs to provide for him, and his younger sister – Maria. She was only six and he felt a deep-seated need to care for her and shield her from harm. Maria's dad was gone too – which made Lil' Q feel responsible for her as a father, less like a big brother. It also made him question why the men his mom seemed to find, didn't love her. He vowed that he would never be the type of man his mother seemed to find.

The weight of his responsibilities settled heavily on his small shoulders as he laid in bed replaying his day.

"Yo, where your pops at?" Lil' Q recalled from yet another stand off earlier in the streets with Marcus.

The question had hit Lil' Q like a punch to the gut. Every time he thought he was used to it, it still stung. Marcus, about two years older than him and one of the kids from the block, had stood there smirking, his Die Heart1 shoes scuffing the concrete. Ever since Lil' Q had lost his temper with Marcus before about this same topic, he was looking for any reason to taunt Lil' Q for a reaction.

"None of yo' business," Lil' Q had shot back, his voice steady despite the tremor in his chest. He adjusted his polo and shrugged his shoulders a bit, trying to look unbothered. Apparently, Marcus "knew" more about Lil' Q's dad than he did, and the rumors around him leaving – but Marcus would never have a conversation with him about it. Lil' Q had lost his temper with Marcus one too many times.

He knew that he couldn't let Marcus see him like that again.

"I heard he playin' stepdaddy to some new kids now too, wonder what yo' dusty lookin' ahh Mama gotta say about that," Marcus taunted, drawing laughs from his crew.

Marcus stayed wearing clothes that was faded but loved to call other folks dusty. Lil' Q could his jawline clinch as just thinking about it. He knew it was pointless to respond, but he was pushing the limits. But Marcus, being Marcus, would have another insult tomorrow and the next day. At least this day he had the confidence to hold his head high and walk away. Sooner or later, he feared, he'd have to do something drastic to push back.

It brought him back to the day he first met Marcus.

July 2, 2023

One afternoon, while sitting on the steps of Lil' Q's building, he and some classmates saw a group of kids approached. Leading them — a tall and lanky guy named Marcus. He wore an oversized wife beater, baggy jeans low enough to match the green bandana on his wrist. His eyes swept over Lil' Q and April like he was sizing them up.

"Y'all new around here?" Marcus asked, his tone flat but edged with something else challenge, maybe.

"Yeah, we just moved in last month," Lil' Q replied, forcing confidence into his voice.

Marcus folded his arms, smirking. *"Fresh meat better watch their step around here."*

Lil' Q stiffened, but April beat him to it. *"We'll be just fine,"* she said, her voice steady.

Marcus held her gaze for a second longer before he let out a low chuckle. *"We'll see about that."*

The group sauntered off, laughing among themselves. Lil' Q let out a slow breath, his hands clenched into fists.

April nudged him. *"Relax. He's just trying to scare us."*

"Yeah, well… it worked, a lil'. I've seen guys like that in the 'hood – you can't trust 'em. They're unpredictable." Lil' Q admitted, shaking his head.

April grinned. *"We'll handle it. We got each other."*

Lil' Q exhaled and nodded. *"Yeah. Always."*

His eyes drifted to a father and son walking past, sharing a bag of chips. The boy reached for another handful, and the father playfully pulled the bag away, laughing before handing it back. Lil' Q watched them until they disappeared down the block.

"You ever wonder what it's like?" he asked.

April raised an eyebrow. *"What what's like?"*

"Having both parents around. Being… normal."

April snorted. *"Normal? In this hood? That's like finding a unicorn that poops rainbow ice cream."*

Lil' Q let out a startled laugh. "Uggghh …. *mane, you wild for that one*."

"*For real though*," April's voice softened. "*Maybe we ain't got what others got, but we got each other. That counts for something.*"

Lil' Q nodded, watching Maria chase bubbles in the small compact yard. "*Yeah. That's something.*"

Chapter 2:

Where Yo' Pops At?

Hearing his mother in the kitchen, Lil' Q decided to get up and have a talk with her. He stood in the kitchen doorway, watching his mom wash the dishes he'd told her he was going to do. He had totally forgotten. He felt bad about it but knew better to offer now. There was something more pressing on his mind anyway. The question burned in his throat, but he needed to break the ice.

"*Ma...*"

"*Mm-hmm*?" She didn't turn around, her hands moving mechanically through the soapy water.

"*Why you don't ever talk about Pops?*"

The sponge slowed. Then stopped. A plate slipped.

"*Some stories...*" she finally said quietly, with a shrug, "*ain't ready to be told.*"

"Yeah... but *you know anything about him raising another family in this 'hood.? I'm just sayin' – I ain't tryna run into the nig-*", he pressed.

"Quin. Washington." she started, her voice shifting from a quiet, patient tone to an irritated, elevated one.

"*Ok Ma',*" he answered quietly, understanding exactly what that meant. They wouldn't talk about. It would end up another conversation that they just couldn't have. Just like the conversation about Maria.

Lil' Q put his head down and walked out of the room, silently taking a light punch at the wall, wishing she knew the pain and resentment she was causing. "*I'm old enough to take matters into my own hands,*" he thought.

He walked back to his room and decided to see if April was sitting outside. It was close to the time the lights would be coming on, so it was too late to see her.

April Martinez was Lil' Q's best friend. She was a firecracker of a girl with curly hair that bounced when she walked and a laugh that was contagious. April lived with her grandmother, who everyone called Abuela, in the apartment across the street from Lil' Q. April's dad had passed away years ago, which put her mom in different work situations. They were fairly new to the city too but Mrs. Martinez was working in another city and April barely got to see her. Lil' Q and April bonded over their shared experiences of loss and the strength they found in their families.

Both families were still adjusting to the new environment, trying to make sense of their small, cluttered apartments and the unfamiliar streets. They both missed their old schools and friends, but knew they had to make the best of their new situation.

For Lil' Q and April, the way they could connect on so much made them feel like they had known each other forever. Even their first meeting was one of those rare moments where everything clicked, and an instant relationship was formed. It was like something had placed them together in this new environment specifically for each other.

June 12. 2023

One day, in the building's narrow walkway. Lil' Q was lugging a box of books up the stairs when he tripped and the books fell all over the ground. April, who was passing by, immediately bent down to help him.

"Hey, clumsy, okay?" she asked, picking up a book and handing it to him.

Lil' Q looked up, embarrassed but grateful. "*Yeah, thanks. Just rather carry all these books in one trip that's all.*" He sat the stack down to get the book from April he'd dropped.

"*I'm Quin but all my friends call me Lil' Q,*" he said, introducing himself.

"April," she replied with a smile. "So would your friends call me Lil' A?" she teased, laughing sarcastically.
Lil' Q wasn't sure whether the stranger was throwing a joke or serious, and his awkward silence must have made her uncomfortable.

"So, you must've just moved in?" she asked, ignoring her previous question, shifting her body weight uncomfortably.

"Yeah, with my mom and sister. It's... a lot to get used to," Lil' Q admitted.

"I hear you. We moved here not too long ago as well, about three months ago. It's different from what I'm used to, it's ok," April said encouragingly.

"Well, I hope you're right. I've been here two days and it's been the worst two days of my life," he said, sitting down on the stair step. Organically, April sat down too, asking about his days. What began as chaos and frustration, ended with peace and a much-needed conversation for them both.

A few days later, wandering through the park, Lil' Q and April noticed a group of kids about their age, all wearing green bandannas. They seemed to be everywhere, hanging out in corners, sitting on stoops, and even playing ball in the park.

"Why you think they're all wearing those green bandannas?" Lil' Q asked, curiosity piqued.

April shrugged. "I don't know. Maybe it's some kind of club?"

"Maybe," Lil' Q said, though he had a feeling it was something more serious. "We should be careful around them," he warned April, while subconsciously being intrigued by the presence of other boys in the neighborhood.

"Definitely," April agreed. "We'll watch each other's backs, right?"

Lil' Q smiled. "Always," putting his arm around her, but looking over his shoulder at the group of boys who'd all stopped mid-movement to watch him and April walk off. That intrigued feeling he had instantly left, and a wave of uneasiness settled in the bottom of his stomach.

From that moment on, Lil' Q and April were inseparable. They spent their afternoons exploring the neighborhood, navigating the cracked sidewalks and graffiti-covered walls. The neighborhood was rough, but it had its own kind of charm. Aside from the park down the street where kids played basketball, a community center offered a glimmer of hope amidst the chaotic nights filled with gunshots and sirens.

Chapter 3:

The Invitation

As the weeks passed, the end of the school year was nearing and Lil' Q and April faced their share of challenges. Lil' Q's mom was constantly exhausted from working longer hours, which meant that he had to take on more responsibility of looking after Maria. April helped out where she could, watching Maria while Lil' Q ran errands or finished his homework, but it still was just too much for a twelve-year-old boy.

At April's apartment, things were equally tough. Abuela was doing her best to find a new job, but the stress was taking a toll on her. She often worried about the bills and whether they would be able to stay in their home or end up moving again. April tried to be strong for her grandmother, but it was hard not to feel the burden of their situation. She couldn't help but to wonder if she'd have to resort to *other* measures again to help the family to keep a roof over their head.

Despite their challenges, Lil' Q and April found joy in their friendship and the possibilities their neighborhood offered. Since their home responsibilities kept them in the house through the week a lot, they discovered a small library within the community center that offered resources online. With the government benefits, both April and Lil' Q had access to internet so they could spend hours reading and talking about their dreams for the future. Lil' Q wanted to be a basketball player like Anthony Edwards, and April dreamed of becoming a writer like the great Lorraine Hansberry.

On the weekends, they were able to spend out in the neighborhood more. As they walked back from the library one Saturday afternoon, the heat slapped the city with a sweltering palm. They decided to take a break near the basketball court but soon found themselves shooting hoops on the cracked court at the end of their street. The sound of sneakers scraping pavement and the rhythmic bounce of the ball mixed with the chatter of kids hanging around them.

A commotion near the fence caught Lil' Q's eye, and he slowly paused mid-dribble. A small crowd had gathered, voices rising in excitement.

"Yo, check it," April murmured, jerking her chin toward two older boys crouched near the fence, throwing dice. Bills flashed between fingers, quick and greedy.

"Seven! Pay up!" a deep voice boomed, followed by groans and laughter.

Lil' Q's feet stayed planted, but his eyes locked onto the roll of bills in one man's hand—thick, heavy. That much money could cover their rent. Buy Maria some new shoes. Maybe even—

"Lil' Q." April's voice snapped like a whip.

His head jerked toward her and shot her the ball quickly.

"Don't even think about it," she muttered, catching the ball quickly. *"You know what happened to Papi."*

Lil' Q swallowed hard. April never talked in detail about her father, but when she did, her voice took on that hard, distant edge. He knew pieces of the story— gambling, debts, wrong people, wrong time, jail time. Now she felt abandoned and overwhelmed by the pressure of feeling like she should be helping in some kind of way.

"*My bad,*" he said, bumping her shoulder playfully, trying to shake the heaviness from the air. "*You right. Besides, I got better things to do than watch grown men throw their rent money away.*"

Lil' Q knew could hear his Mama's, "*Everything that glitter ain't gold,*" warning. Those men looked like they were getting money, but he knew it didn't come without a price. He wasn't sure if that was a price he was willing to pay.

"*Like what? Losing to me in 21?*" April smirked, bringing his attention back to the court. She ran up the court to layup but missed.

"*Girl, please! You couldn't score on me if the hoop was twice as wide.*"

Their laughter cut through the thick heat as they started their game again. Behind them, the dice game continued, its clatter an uneasy rhythm beneath their fun.

A deep, steady voice rang out across the court. "*Hey, y'all! Need a third player?*"

They turned to see a man — tall, broad-shouldered, calm but commanding. A whistle hung from his neck, swaying slightly as he stepped forward. His eyes held weight, the kind that knew things — maybe too much.

April glanced at Lil' Q.

Lil' Q shrugged and tossed him the ball. "*You hoop?*"

He caught it one-handed and smiled. *"Som' like that,"* he said, catching the ball and instantly getting in front of Lil' Q defensively.

They played. Not long, but long enough for stranger to size them up. He didn't talk much — didn't need to. His eyes did the work. Observing. Calculating. Waiting.

After the final shot fell, he wiped sweat from his brow and nodded toward the street. *"Y'all ever been to the community center on 43rd? The Garvey Center?"*

They shook their heads, yes, at the same time.

"Y'all know the summer program starts June 1st. Sports. Music. Film. Writing. Real skills."

"How much to join?" April asked.

The stranger answered, *"Absolutely free for kids in the area."*

Lil' Q didn't sound the like of that.

"Don't non' follow free in this neighborhood but trouble," he spoke, disappointed.

"Not over here, the program is new with new facilitators," the man corrected, *"We just want to offer real chances. For people who got somethin' in them."*

April narrowed her eyes. *"And you think we got that?"*

He stepped closer. His voice dropped just enough to shift the mood. *"Let's just say... I don't show up to random courts for no reason. And you can Call me Coach J."*

He turned and walked off, leaving the ball bouncing quietly behind him.

Lil' Q stood frozen. *"Yo. What just happened?"*

April watched him disappear into the city heat, her arms crossed, jaw tight.

"I don't know," she murmured. *"But I got a feeling that man ain't just teaching free throws."*

Chapter 4:
Is There Hope?

Two weeks later…

Lil' Q often thought about his dad. The memories came in scattered pieces—fleeting glimpses he tried to hold onto, like catching fireflies in a jar. He could still feel the rough stubble on his father's chin when he carried him on his shoulders at the carnival, smell the buttery popcorn in the air, hear the distant laughter of families blending into the night. But the memories never stayed. They slipped away as quickly as they came, leaving behind an ache he couldn't quite name.

That evening, as he sat on the stoop of their building, staring at the cracks in the pavement, his mom stepped outside and settled beside him. Without a word, she wrapped an arm around his shoulders, pulling him close.

"*You know, Pops loves you very much*," she murmured.

Lil' Q nodded but kept his gaze ahead. He didn't trust his voice. He wouldn't cry. Not in front of her. Not when she was already carrying so much.

His mom sighed, her fingers gently rubbing his back. "*I know things have been hard, but we're going to be okay. We have each other.*"

Lil' Q let out a slow breath and leaned his head against her shoulder, letting the warmth of her presence push back the loneliness. She was right. They had each other. They had to be okay.

Across the street, on her grandmother's porch, April sat on the swing, absently watching the sky fade from orange to indigo. It had been months since her mother left for work in another city, but it still felt like yesterday. Some nights, she could still hear her mom humming in the kitchen or feel the warmth of her arms after a long day. But then the memories would slip away, leaving nothing but silence.

Her grandmother must have sensed the heaviness in her chest because she sat beside her and started rubbing small, slow circles on her back—the same way she did when April was little.

"Tu mamá te extraña, ¿sabes?", Abuela said.

April swallowed hard and nodded. Her grandmother just reminded her that her mother missed her. She wanted to cry. She wouldn't cry. She had to be strong. For herself. For her grandmother.

"*She's working hard for us*," her grandmother continued, her voice steady. "*And she'll be home soon. In the meantime, we have, each other,"* she pointed between the two. *"And we're gonna get through this. Together."*

April exhaled, allowing herself to lean into her grandmother's side; finally letting the tears flow. The steady rhythm of Abuela's breathing was comforting, grounding. Maybe she was right. Maybe they'd be okay.

As she sat there, another memory surfaced—one from the early days of her friendship with Lil' Q.

Almost like clockwork, Lil' Q yelled from across the street, speaking to Abuela. When he did, Abuela spoke back and then went back into the apartment.

April continued to sway gently on her porch swing, not really feeling like walking across the street. They caught each other's eye, hesitated, then waved—awkward, uncertain.

Then, without thinking, Lil' Q puffed out his cheeks and crossed his eyes in an exaggerated, ridiculous face.

April snorted, then fired back by sticking out her tongue and scrunching her nose. A silent challenge.

Lil' Q raised an eyebrow. Oh, it was on.

For the next few minutes, they exchanged the silliest, most outrageous faces they could muster, each trying to outdo the other. Until, finally, they both cracked, bursting into laughter that echoed through the quiet evening.

When the laughter died down, Lil' Q called across the street, "*So… how was your day*?"

April shrugged. "*Typical. Yours*?"

Lil' Q smirked.

"*Where's Maria*?" April yelled.

"*Over at Shante house wit' her lil' sister*," Lil' Q said.

Lil' Q didn't have a lot of time before he'd have to set the table, but he decided to walk and visit April for a little while.

April's smile softened as he sat beside her.

"*I miss my mom a lot*," she blurted, holding her tears.

"*I miss my dad too,*" he responded quietly, choking back his own tears, "*It's like. like. Parents don't give a care in the world about the decisions they make,*" he said colder, anger budding.

For a moment, neither of them spoke. Then, out of the corner of his eye, Lil' Q noticed a church bus picking up a family. It was a Wednesday evening, of course. That meant the Porch Patrol would all be heading to Bible Study.

"*My mom prays a lot,*" he said suddenly, inspired, remembering the days where his family went to Sunday services.

April turned toward him, curiosity flickering in her eyes. "*Really?*"

Lil' Q nodded. "*She says it makes her feel whole. Gives her peace.*"

April sat with that for a moment. "*I've never seen Mamá pray. Maybe I should try it.*"

"*It might help,*" Lil' Q said. "*And even if it doesn't… at least it's something you can say you tried to do.*"

April tapped her chin, pretending to think. Then, she grinned. "*You'd pray with me?*"

Lil' Q chuckled. "*I mean… yeah, I guess.*"

"*Cool.*" April smiled, leaning back against the swing. "*We'll give it a shot.*"

They sat there for a short while, sharing stories, dreams, and quiet moments in between. And somehow, during all the uncertainty, the loneliness felt a little less heavy.

Maybe they couldn't change their circumstances. But they could keep dreaming. Keep pushing forward. And they weren't alone.

Chapter 5:
Euphoria

The screen of April's phone lit up her face in the darkness of her bedroom. It was 3:00 AM, and sleep wasn't coming. Her Euphoria feed was full of happy families – ending the school year with mothers and daughters at the mall, end of the year dances, perfect little squares of lives she couldn't touch.

"*Ape, you still up*?" Lil' Q's text popped up, "*Can't sleep. Too many thoughts.*"

"*You can't be wantin to talk to me this late calling me Ape.*

"*Stop playing mane… you like that nickname. I'm the only one that can call you that… but so ... you up.*"

April didn't feel like a playful back and forward, ignoring Lil' Q's teasing she replied, "*"Yeah, I'm up. These Euphoria stories got me feeling some type of way* 💀"

April smiled, but it didn't reach her eyes. Her thumb hovered over her mom's old Euphoria profile - frozen in time from six months ago. The last post was still there: "*Sometimes the hardest choices are the only choices we have. Love you, mi vida* 🤍"

April 2021

"*Mamá, why do we have to move?*" April had asked that day, watching her mother pack frantically.

"*Mi amor, sometimes...*" her mom's hands trembled as she folded clothes, "*sometimes people we trust aren't who they say they are.*"

"Is this about Papí?" April's voice had dropped to a whisper.

Her mother had frozen, just for a second. *"Your father... he's not..."* She'd stopped, shaking her head. *"Just know that everything I do, everything I've ever done, is to protect you."*

April had noticed the unopened letter on the dresser, postmarked from a prison in Texas. She never asked about it. Shortly after that, all she was told was that her father was dead.

"Yo, you see what Marcus posted?" Lil' Q's text snapped April back to reality.

She switched to his page and there it was - a photo of her posing with her purse and shades on from yesterday, caught at a bad angle, caption reading: *"Somebody tell this broke girl to stop frontin' like she got it like that with that knock off purse. 😂"*

Comments were already piling up:
💬 *"Fr fr 💀"*

"Expensive purse but dusty uniforms? 👀 Yeah right!" 💬

💬 *"Lyin' like her mama work outta town 😴 she outta town aight - out on somebody corner!"*

"She be hangin' with that lil' boy that don't never have his hair cut. They both look like some lames." 💬

April's fingers shook as she typed: "*Delete this.*"

"*Or what?* 🐽" Marcus replied instantly.

Lil' Q jumped in: "*Bro take it down fr fr. This ain't cool.*"

April watched as Lil' Q started defending her in the comments, but the damage was done. Screenshots would be forever whether he deleted it or not.

Her phone buzzed with a DM from Lil' Q:

"*Don't let them get to you. They don't know nothing about us.*"

She clicked on Lil' Q's profile - his latest post showed him grinning with his little sister at the park, caption: "*Living my best life* 🏀 "

But April knew the truth. Behind that smile was a kid who'd eaten nothing but ramen for dinner three nights straight so his sister could have a meal with meat and vegetables.

"*It's wild,*" she texted back. "*How everyone's living their highlight reel while we're just trying to make it through the director's cut.*"

"*Facts* 💯 *But hey, at least we keepin' it real. Unlike Marcus flexing them fake Js today trying to hide them dollar store laces like he got it like that.* 😂"

April laughed for real this time, the sound echoing in her quiet room. Her eyes drifted to the small box under her bed where she kept her mom's things - including that mysterious letter she never opened. Sometimes she wondered if her father really was dead like everyone said. The way her mom used to tense up whenever his name came up, the whispered phone calls in Spanish, the sudden move to Abuela's...

Her phone lit up again. This time it was an old photo memory: her mom braiding her hair in their old kitchen, both of them laughing. The caption read: "*Your past may be painful, but it doesn't define your future.* 🙏"

She typed back to Lil' Q: "*You ever feel like there's more to your story than what everybody tells you*?"

"*Every single day. But the real always recognize the real* 💪."

April smiled, closing Euphoria and opening her notes app.

She started typing:

"Dear Mamá,

There's so much I want to ask you. About Papí. About why you left. About the letters you hide..."

The words flowed easier in the dark, when nobody was watching, when she could just be herself - not the tough girl at school, not the grateful granddaughter, just April, trying to make sense of her story.

Chapter 6:
Elevate You

Coach J had always cared deeply about his community. With his shaved head and thick beard, he looked like a gentle giant, someone who could command respect with just a look but chose to win hearts with his warm smile. He had grown up in Benton Heights, the same neighborhood, playing basketball on the cracked courts and dreaming of a future beyond the city's limits.

Basketball had been his escape route. The game took him through high school, then college, and brought him full circle—right back to the same streets that raised him. Now, degree in hand and vision in his heart, Coach J was ready to give back.

He never forgot his own mentor, Coach Kabe—a man who saw light in him when all others saw was trouble. That influence stuck with him. Life. Respect. Self-belief. Now, Coach J was determined to pass those same lessons on.

The Garvey Center had become his second home. Every day, he saw the same struggles he had faced as a kid—poverty, broken families, and the lure of the streets. But he also saw hope in the eyes of the children who walked through the doors, kids who, like him, needed someone to believe in them.

The Elevate You Summer Enrichment Program was his next move.

Coach J had been looking for potential the entire year before that and slowly built a team of prospects through the neighborhoods. He was hoping they showed up after personally introducing himself to each.

Each summer, he saw more kids fall between the cracks. Bright eyes dulled by the streets. Futures snatched by bad timing and worse choices. But he believed—truly believed—that all it took was one steady voice, one positive outlet, one reason to believe they mattered. That's why he spent months recruiting face to face. Walking to parks. Sitting on stoops. Meeting parents. Leaving flyers at churches and corner stores.

This morning, those seeds were blooming.

As he stepped into the community center's basketball court, he couldn't help but feel a wave gratitude and purpose.

Its fluorescent lights flickered intermittently, casting a stark, artificial glow over the polished hardwood court. The scent of sweat and old gym socks clung to the air, mingling with the faint hint of floor polish. The court gleamed under the light, each bounce of the ball a heartbeat.

One of his favorite prospects, Lil' Q, was already on the floor. He dribbled with precision, his off-brand black-and-whites squeaking rhythmically. From the smudged glass near the entrance, a shadow passed. Tall. Broad. Hoodie up. Green bandanna poking from the pocket like a flag of warning.

Michael Adams.

"*Yo, you good*?" April's voice cut through the moment, low and steady, her dark eyes scanning his face. She had her hands on her hips, her signature ponytail swaying slightly with each breath. Sweat glistened on her temple from their last drill, but her gaze stayed sharp, focused.

Before he could answer, Coach J's voice boomed across the court.

"'*Ight, young kings and queens! Let's run some plays.!*"

Lil' Q looked again — Michael was still watching. Too still. Too quiet.

Coach J, somehow always two steps ahead, addressed the gym like he was reading minds.

"*If you're not part of this program, I need you off these premises.*"

Michael vanished with the others older guys who didn't belong.

April shot Lil' Q a look. "*That man's not just running drills. He's watching the whole board.*"

Lil' Q nodded, his eyes drifting back to the now-empty entrance.

And for a moment, it felt like safety had a name—and it started with "Coach."

As the drills wrapped and the gym's energy cooled, the sound of sneakers faded into shuffles and whispers. Basketballs stopped bouncing. Water bottles hissed open. The buzz of movement slowed to something softer—almost sacred. Lil' Q lingered near the folding chairs, helping Coach J stack them against the wall. His arms moved, but his ears stayed open.

That's when he heard her — **Tasha Carter**.

She stood behind the front desk like it was her personal runway, flipping through permission slips like they were VIP invites to the hottest event in Benton Heights. Her voice carried that signature mix of authority and sparkle that made teachers, students, and even parents pause to listen.

"*I'm telling you*," she whispered loudly to Ms. Jenkins, her acrylics clicking against the countertop, "*Michael ain't always been about that life. You remember when he used to hoop here, right*?"

Lil' Q's ears perked up like radar.

Tasha Carter? Talking about Michael?

That wasn't just anybody running her mouth.
Tasha was *that girl*.

The girl whose name stayed in everybody's mouth for a reason. Freshman Class President. Captain of the JV Cheer Squad. The closest thing Benton Heights had to royalty. Her hair? Always laid. Her shoes? Always matching the fit. Her phone? Buzzing nonstop with group chats full of the city's who's-who. Even the elementary schoolers whispered when she walked by.

But she wasn't just pretty or popular—Tasha had pull. Real pull.

Her dad owned **Carter's Convenience**, the neighborhood cornerstone on 45th and Maple. If it happened in Benton Heights, it either started in that store, got talked about in that store, or ended with somebody storming out that store.

Ms. Jenkins adjusted her glasses, letting out a sigh that felt like it carried years of unspoken history.

Chapter 7:
Carter's Watch

Tasha Carter hadn't spoken to Michael Adams in over two years — not since her brother Dre stopped bringing him around.

Dre and Michael were tight once. The kind of tight that came from long summer days on the blacktop and late-night walks home from the corner store. They used to be inseparable hooping at The Garvey Center, sharing video games and phones, dreaming of college ball like it was already written.

But then something shifted.

Michael changed.

Started showing up to their house late, with bruised knuckles and a smirk that didn't match the boy she once knew. Dre didn't say much, just stopped bringing him around. The silence between them said more than words ever could. Tasha noticed. She always noticed. Especially the day Dre came home with that split lip and told their daddy he "fell." And when she asked their dad asked what happened, Mr. Carter just said, *"He chose the block."*

Tasha never forgot that line.

So, when she spotted Michael posted near the gym wall, before training, the past rushed back in waves. He wasn't just a former friend of her brother's—he was a walking reminder of what went wrong.

And a bittersweet memory of what could happen when things went just right.

Two summers ago…

The buzz of the corner store's old neon sign flickered against the dark sky. Benton Heights was alive that night—music thumping from a party down the block, laughter echoing off brick walls, and the smell of barbecue lingering in the air like smoke and secrets.

Tasha shoved her hands in the pocket of her pants, her throat still hot from the shouting match with Dre. Her feet led her without thinking—past Carter's Convenience, across 45th, toward the only store still open.

"Yo," a voice called out, smooth and familiar.

Tasha turned. Michael stepped from the shadows near the vending machine, a grape soda in one hand and a Honey Bun in the other.

"Michael?" she asked, startled.

"What you doin' out this late, Lil' Carter?" he smirked. "Ain't Dre gon' have a fit?"

She scoffed and rolled her eyes. "Don't call me that and forget Dre. He act like my daddy instead of my brother. I hate him right now."

Michael raised an eyebrow, cracking open his soda. "He care. Just don't know how to show it all the time."

Tasha leaned against the brick wall beside him, arms crossed. "Why I ain't seen you lately?"

Michael hesitated. "Things... changed."

"Why?"

He took a sip before answering. "Sometimes people gotta choose between what's easy and what's right. I didn't choose right let yo Daddy tell it."

She looked up at him. "I'm glad of all people I saw you. Why you out tonight?"

"I dunno. Maybe I was hopin' for a different kind of night."

They stood in silence for a beat, the only sound being a motorcycle revving in the distance. Then Tasha asked the question that had been burning in her chest.

"You ever feel like... nobody sees you unless you mess up?"

Michael glanced over, his eyes softer now. "Every day. But you? You different. You walk in a room and people listen—even if they pretend not to."

She looked down, a shy smile tugging at her lips. "You just sayin' that."

"Nah," he said, stepping closer. "I see you, Tasha."

She looked up—and before she could second-guess it, before her nerves could catch up—he leaned in. Their lips met in a clumsy, quiet kiss. No fireworks. No music. Just shared breath and unsaid stories.

When they pulled back, Tasha's heart thumped loud in her ears.

"I should get home," she whispered.

"Yeah," he said, backing up, eyes never leaving hers.
"I'll walk you."

They didn't talk much on the way back, but something
passed between them—something unspoken and
unforgettable.

By the next week, Michael was gone.

But that night stayed folded in the back of Tasha's
memory—creased, hidden, but never erased.

And now, seeing him again — older, darker, still
carrying that storm behind his eyes — made her feel
exposed in a way she hated.

She tightened her grip on the permission slips in front
of her, flipping through them like shields. Every kid on
that list was someone she wanted to keep safe—from
the world, and from the ghosts that had once haunted
her own block.

As if in her thoughts still about Michael, she realized
Ms. Jenkins was still talking.

"*Mm-hmm. Before what happened to his mama... that
boy had game. Could've gone D1 if...*" Ms. Jenkins'
voice trailed off, and her eyes did the rest of the
talking.

Lil' Q, still ear hustlin', paused mid-stack, the metal
chair cold and steady in his hand. Michael?
Basketball dreams? It didn't line up with the image he
knew—the cold stare, the green bandanna, the street
whispers. But that's the thing about stories... they got
layers.

A glow caught Lil' Q's eye.

Marcus strolled past with his phone in hand.

"What's up Big M," he heard Marcus answer, looking around to check his surroundings before lowering his voice. **Big M**. That had to be Michael's contact name.

The streets had long arms, and apparently, they stretched all the way into the gym.

Tasha's voice rose just enough to break through the buzz of conversations left from those still waiting for their parents. No longer a whisper—now a public service announcement.

"*Well, they just better know this summer ain't for him or his boys,*" she said, tossing her hair back with a flick. "*This is a respectful facility. For kids who got some home training.*"

Lil' Q's stomach twisted. April, sitting nearby tying her shoes, raised an eyebrow. She caught every word too.

Ms. Jenkins tried to step in, her voice calm. "*Tasha, Coach J got this. Trust me.*"

Tasha didn't flinch. Her ponytail of locs swayed like punctuation as she stood tall behind the desk. She glanced around the gym, catching the eyes that were already watching her as they left. She didn't like loose ends. And Michael Adams?

He was one.

The kind that unraveled things from the inside out. She knew all too well.

"*Well, if he don't...*" she paused, her gaze sharp as glass, "*...my daddy do.*"

The gym fell quiet for a beat. Not because folks agreed—but because when Tasha Carter spoke like that, people knew she wasn't bluffing.

Chapter 8:
Marcus the Menace

Lil' Q bent to grab the next chair, but his mind stayed behind in the gym. Something about this summer felt...off. And it was just getting started.

By the time Lil' Q stepped outside, the night air had cooled — considering the humid Mississippi heat, but his thoughts hadn't. That last exchange at the gym clung to him like sweat on his skin. Tasha's words, Marcus's phone call, and Michael's shadow — none of it sat right. The lines were starting to blur. And as much as he wanted to believe the Elevate You program was a safe zone… it felt like something — or someone — was slipping through the cracks.

"*Ready amigo,*" April asked, walking out of the door.

"*Sí,*" he playfully answered.

"*Yo, let's go to Carter's,*" he said, inspired by seeing Tasha.

The evening air was thick with the lingering warmth of the day, the scent of fried food and exhaust drifting from the nearby takeout spot. Streetlights flickered on one by one, casting long shadows over the cracked sidewalk as Lil' Q and April made their way to the store. Their sneakers scuffed against the pavement, the sounds of the neighborhood filling the quiet between them—cars rolling by with bass-heavy music, laughter spilling from a nearby stoop, the occasional bark of a restless dog.

As they neared the corner store, a sudden commotion caught their attention. Two younger kids were shoving each other near the curb, their voices sharp with frustration. Then, cutting through the noise, came a voice steady with authority.

"*Ay yo!*" Michael's tone was firm but controlled, carrying weight without force. "*We don't do that here. Y'all got a problem? Talk it out or take it somewhere else.*"

The kids froze under his gaze, tension dissolving almost instantly. Without another word, they scattered, their quick retreat more out of respect than fear. Lil' Q, mid-step, slowed during passing by as Michael turned, catching his stare. There was no smirk, no posturing—just a slight nod, a quiet acknowledgment.

"*That's how you handle business,*" Michael said, his voice pitched just loud enough for Lil' Q to hear. "*No violence needed. Sometimes just being heard is enough.*"

Lil' Q's jaw tightened. **That wasn't what he expected.** Michael wasn't just out here keeping the peace — he had control, a different kind of power. One that didn't come from fear, but from something deeper.

April, shifting beside him, tugged at his sleeve. "*Come on,*" she whispered, urgency laced in her voice.

There was something about the way she said it, the quick glance she shot toward Michael, that made Lil' Q wonder if she knew something he didn't.

Then, behind them, another voice entered the mix. Marcus. Lil' Q looked back to see him approaching Michael, phone in hand, his posture relaxed but his words laced with curiosity.

"*Yo, Big Mike, for real though, why you even care about these little kids*?" he asked. Lil' Q glanced back to see that Michael and Marcus were walking behind them, probably going to Carter's too.

Michael's response came without hesitation, his voice measured, grounded. "*Because nobody cared when I was their age. Sometimes the streets raise you, but that don't mean they gotta raise everybody.*"

Lil' Q's fingers curled at his sides. That feeling was back—the same one he'd had at the gym, when he learned Michael could've been something different. **Like an itch under his skin, a question he couldn't quite shake.**

Michael wasn't just watching. He wasn't just existing on the edges. He was choosing to be something else.

And Lil' Q wasn't sure why, but he needed to understand why that mattered so much.

"*I see ya April,*" Michael hollered behind them.

Throwing a shot that could kill over her shoulder, April yelled, "*effffff you man.*"

"*Aye we can handle that, one way or another,*" Marcus snapped back, eyes narrowing.

April looked at Lil' Q, hopeless.

"*I keep telling you stop popping off at the mouth to that mane,*" Lil' Q warned her.

"*Tsk..shhiiii, ok,*" April tossed back, with a look of agitation. As Lil' Q and April approached the convenient store's door, Michael and Marcus walked in behind them.

"*Yo, bet I hit that,*" Marcus said to Michael, just loud enough for them to overhear.

"*Chill out with all that,*" Michael said.

"*Son, I've told you more than once, - don't come in here wearin' just that wife beater.*"

Mr. Carter had come from his office to address Marcus, who only responded with a threatening and intimidating stare.

Michael whistled, motioning for Marcus to leave, throwing the bag of chips he had in his hand on the floor.

"*It's more than one way to handle ol' Uncle Tom ahh ol' folks like that … trust me,*" said Michael in a calm, playful tone.

Lil' Q and April exchanged a concerned look, while checking out their drinks and hot dogs. Carter's usually had some kind of quick meal, especially for the youngsters.

Lil' Q wondered if Michael had just made a threat or if he was trying to teach Marcus how to control his temper. One thing was for certain to Lil' Q: Marcus Corbin was a neighborhood menace.

As they stepped into the night beginning to dawn, Lil' Q couldn't tell if they'd just dodged something dangerous … or stepped deeper into it.

Chapter 9:
The Block is Hot

Walking home, Lil' Q and April were silent.

Lil' Q was thinking of how to warn April about mouthing off to dudes like Marcus while April was also thinking about her own safety.

"*April, you can't be popping off at dudes like Marcus,*" he said, glancing around. "*I know you think you tough, but that kind of tough can get you hurt.*"

"*I got some for somebody like Marcus,*" she said stubbornly.

"*Aight, forget it,*" Lil' Q said, dropping the topic.

Suddenly, sirens blasted behind them – ambulance and police sped dangerously by them heading in their direction.

April's phone rung and Lil' Q's mother texted him.

"**GO HOME NOW**!!!" the message from his mom displayed on his notifications.

"Abuela," April answered her phone.

As April was listening to her grandmother, she motioned for Lil' Q to walk faster as she started speeding up.

The two rushed to their apartment complex, only to see what appeared to be a crime scene.

Agnes, a faithful member of the Porch Patrol was on a stretcher being placed into the ambulance, as her granddaughter, Tina, was talking to the police officers.

She was crying drastically, with frantic hands everywhere.

Abuela was out on the porch as well when they made it to the block.

"*Abuela!*" April exclaimed.

"*Third robbery this week! Where the police at??*" they overheard a Porch Patrol member saying.

"*Yo, you seeing this?*" Lil' Q said as he turned toward April.

April sucked her teeth, twisting one of her braids. "*My abuela was talking about it just this morning. Said somebody hit the Williams family down the block too. Took everything.*"

"*You kids. Must be careful this summer. Too many things. Happening.*" Abuela said, shaking her head, and murmuring as she went back into the house.

"*Yo, I gotta get this food on before my moms gets home. I'll text you,*" Lil' Q said, backing away quickly.

He'd seen enough for the day, and it was all starting to remind him of his other neighborhoods. Why did peace always feel so temporary? He couldn't protect everybody – his mom, Maria, April ...not even himself. Moments like this made him miss his dad most. And hate him, too.

"*How could he just leave a family like that?*" he thought, "*What kinda man does this?*"

At the same time, as much as he hated to admit – a large part of him wanted him there. The truth was, the question that plagued Lil' Q the most was – who was going to protect him?

Inside of the Martinez residence, April and Abuela sat down for their favorite meal of the week. It was the first of the month, which meant that the government's food benefits card was loaded and Abuela had a fully stocked pantry and 'fridge.

The first of the month were like holidays to them because they could enjoy the most expensive meals they liked.

Tonight, Abuela had made **chiles en nogada**— poblano peppers stuffed with picadillo, smothered in a creamy walnut sauce, and sprinkled with bright red pomegranate seeds. The dish was as colorful as it was sacred, a traditional labor of love that Abuela only pulled out for special occasions.

April grinned as she took her first bite, the sweet-savory blend melting on her tongue.

"*Abuela, you snapped on this one,*" she said, her mouth still half full. "*You sure you didn't steal this recipe from a restaurant in Puebla?*"

Abuela chuckled, dabbing her mouth with a cloth napkin. "*Mija, Puebla learned from me. This recipe has been in our family since before you were born. Your bisabuela used to make it with goat meat, back in Durango.*"

April let the flavors linger, her eyes trailing to the bright papel picado banners still hanging over the kitchen table. The warmth of the food, the scent of cinnamon and clove, and the soft hum of boleros playing from the old radio made the apartment feel like a sanctuary—at least for the night.

"*I can't wait until we can eat like this every night,*" April said, sighing.

Abuela raised an eyebrow. "*Well, walnuts are forty-eight pesos a bag, and pomegranates are bougie now,*" she replied, smirking. "*And even if we don't ever to get to eat like this every night – at least once a month, we remind ourselves—our culture is rich, even if our wallets ain't.*"

April, "*If I got a job, we could,*" she said – reminding her Abuela that she'd offered to help many times.

"*No, no,*" Abuela immediately cried, "*We will be different here. Good education. Then husband,*" she continued in between bites.

"*ABUELA!*" April groaned.

Abuela looked at her and seemed to stare into her soul.

"*You know the plan, Mija,*" she said quietly, "*You know the plan.*"

There was nothing left for April to say. In their culture, the plan was the plan. There was no need to argue but April was intent on not putting herself in the same position as her mother.

They had come to America to do things differently, and that's what she planned to do.

April picked her phone up in hesitation and then opened her messages. She went to Marcus' number.

"Are you sure I can take you up on that offer anytime?" she asked.

"Anytime" he immediately responded, with a smirk emoji.

She stared at her half-eaten plate, the flavors suddenly dull. Safety felt like a luxury she couldn't afford anymore. If no one else was going to step in … maybe Marcus could.

And if Abuela's plan wouldn't protect her – she'd start building her own.

Chapter 10:
Down for Me

The next day…

The sun hadn't yet reached its peak, but the gym at The Garvey Center was already buzzing on day two of Elevate You program. Not with basketballs today, but with voices. Coach J stood at center court with a clipboard, his whistle swinging gently around his neck.

"Alright, listen up!" he called out. The chatter died down. *"Today starts our Zone Legacy Projects. This summer ain't just about buckets and drills. We building legacy out here. Real change. Each of y'all is assigned to a zone. Cleanups, murals, even helping the elders."*

Lil' Q leaned on the bleachers beside April, already sensing this day was going to be complicated.

Coach J began calling names. *"Zone Three. Marcus Corbin. April Martinez. Quin Washington."*

April's eyes widened. *"Nah. Nope. Coach, come on."*

Marcus smirked, *"That ain't what you was saying last night on my phone girl."*

Lil' Q shot a look toward Marcus, then April.

Coach J looked up. *"April, this ain't about comfort. This about impact. You three got potential together. You just don't see it yet."*

Before she could respond, another name hit like a brick.

"Annnnd your youth mentor: Michael Adams."

Lil' Q glanced at April. Her mouth opened, then shut. She sat back, shaking her head.

Their **zone** was a worn-down strip near Carter's Convenience — cracked sidewalks of course, overflowing trash cans, and a vandalized park wall begging for a fresh coat of paint. It wasn't just a project site. It was a battleground.

Michael stood at the edge, arms folded, scanning the area like he was looking for something only he could see. April crossed her arms, still fuming.

"*I ain't cleaning nothing next to him,*" she muttered.

Marcus rolled his eyes. "*April why you playin' hard mane.*"

Lil' Q stood between them, broom in hand. "*Can we just start?*"

They worked in awkward silence. Raking, sweeping, tossing junk into bags. The sun crept higher. Tempers shorter.

Then April spotted something.

Behind the park wall, half-buried under a pile of old flyers and soda cans, was a spray-painted tag: a crown with a cracked halo, flanked by unfamiliar initials.

"*What is that?*" she asked.

Michael moved fast. Too fast. He stepped between her and the wall.

"*It's nothing. Just old street stuff.*"

Lil' Q saw his face change — tight. Guarded.

"*Looks recent to me,*" Marcus mumbled, but he said it like he knew.

Michael turned, his voice low. "*Just clean up. Leave that part to me.*"

They obeyed. But Lil' Q couldn't unsee it.

Later that afternoon, as the cleanup wrapped and Marcus and April wandered off to grab a snack, Lil' Q stayed back. He sat near the mural wall, sketchpad in hand, pretending to draw. But his eyes were locked on Michael, who was now alone, wiping down the spray-painted symbol with a rag.

Coach J's voice startled him.

"*You watchin' or workin'?*"

Lil' Q looked up. "*Bit of both.*"

Coach J sat next to him. "*You got good eyes. But use 'em wise. Not everything broken wants to be fixed.*"

Lil' Q didn't respond. He just flipped to a new page in his sketchbook.

And started drawing the cracked crown.

Inside of Carter's Convenience, April and Marcus ducked in as the bell above the door gave its usual jingle. Mr. Carter stood behind the counter, counting singles and eyeing Marcus with suspicion.

April headed toward the refrigerated section, grabbing two sodas and a bag of chips. Marcus loitered near the candy aisle, snatching a bag of Hot Fries with a smirk.

"*You always stare at me like that, old man*?" Marcus barked.

Mr. Carter didn't flinch. "*I stare at trouble.*"

April stepped in quickly. "*Marcus, chill. Let's just go.*"

"*Nah, he got something to say, let him say it,*" Marcus shot back.

Mr. Carter put the money down and walked around the counter. "*You walk in here every time like you own the place. You don't. This is a safe spot. You mess that up, you're out.*"

Marcus laughed, but his eyes didn't. "*Funny how safe don't mean the same thing for everybody.*"

April stood frozen, the tension gripping her chest. "*Let's just leave. Please.*"

Marcus tossed the Hot Fries back on the shelf. "*We out.*"

He pushed open the door harder than necessary. April gave Mr. Carter a quick apologetic glance before following.

She didn't say a word as they walked, her body stiff.

Later that night, when she lay in bed, her phone buzzed with a text.

Marcus: "*Listen? You gon' be down with the kind of work I got for you – you gotta be down for ME on everything!*"

She stared at the screen, now in fear of what she had seemingly gotten herself into with him.

About the Author

La'Kendrick Davis is a passionate author, filmmaker, and entrepreneur dedicated to inspiring spiritual growth and personal transformation. As the visionary behind Witness Legend and founder of Die Heart Productions, he brings a unique perspective shaped by his Delta roots in Greenville, Mississippi.

La'Kendrick is the author of *Pray Personal Journal*, which encourages readers to deepen their prayer life through intentional reflection and devotion. His debut fiction title *8's or 4's?* addresses the critical choices facing at-risk youth navigating challenges like gang violence and peer pressure.

With over a decade of experience in music production and digital media, La'Kendrick combines his creative expertise with his faith-driven mission to help others tell their stories and build lasting legacies. When he's not writing or producing, he's mentoring young entrepreneurs and developing content that bridges the gap between street wisdom and spiritual truth.